The Eve to Believe

Minister Robert D. Loftlin

Fulton Books, Inc.
Meadville, PA

Published by Fulton Books 2021

ISBN 978-1-63710-273-2 (paperback)
ISBN 978-1-63710-274-9 (digital

Printed in the United States of America

To Dad (Walter J. Loftlin Sr.) and Jay (Walter J. Loftlin Jr.),
I love you and miss you both.
This book is dedicated in your memory.

Contents

Acknowledgments

I would like to give special thanks to the people, or my village, that made this book possible. Without you, there would not be a story to tell or, for that matter, me to be here to tell it.

First my Lord and Savior Jesus Christ for His sacrifice for me and the greatest gift I could ever receive, eternal life and peace.

Mommy (Quandora Loftlin) for life, love, and the gift of teaching me to keep learning about Jesus. Your trust in God has been a true inspiration, and I love you.

My big sister Renee Loftlin Laws for being a second mom and business consultant, and her husband, my brother-in-law Phillip, for defending your family as you sacrificed to defend this country.

To my sister-in-law Wanda Loftlin, you loved and supported my oldest brother, Jay, while he was here and the two beautiful daughters you gave him.

My big brother Christopher Loftlin for being a great big brother and hero and his wife, Brianni, for being a good sister to me and being the helpmeet he needed.

My nieces and nephews Quanda [first one] and Shannon Badness Loftlin. Phillip [little bro], Charisse [tater tot], and Thomas [godson T. J.] Laws. I promise no crying, but I watched you all grow and love you all as the blessings my brother and sister gave me.

My great nieces Imani Loftlin and Amore Laws, just remember to follow Christ and learn about Him. The Great-Uncle Bobby loves you and knows you both will make a difference in your generation.

To my wife and helpmeet, Tamara, I have a new life and a heart because of God blessing me with you. There are not enough words to say how much I love you and thank you for being you. I know God answers prayers, and I asked Him to send me an angel, and he did.

To Julian and Corey (James), you will always be my boys, and I do not need any papers to say that. Your support and push is more than appreciated and received.

To the Kay and Bottenger families, my family, thank you for taking me in and including me in all you do. I was and am blessed to laugh, cry, and even get dirty with you (Boro Bombers #1).

Special thanks to Eric, you are the best friend I could ever ask for. A good example of a gentleman is a strong man.

To Paul "Big Bear" Swanger, you believed in the vision and stuck with me throughout the process. You helped to bring this story to life.

To Christopher and Stacy Hunter, my brother and sister in Christ, mentor, teacher, and friend. You are the stability when things were unstable, and you are deliverer of God's word. Much love and respect to you both.

Thank you to Orville Palmer and family for being a part of my village and for your prayers, love, and support.

To Michael Barnes, "Mace," for believing and helping me to get to next level vision with the story.

And finally, the folks at Heaven on Earth Christian Fellowship, Alphonso Dashiell and Siobahn Williams (in memory of Zion Williams). You made this story literally come to life. I truly thank you from the bottom of my heart. My dream became reality because of your unselfish, welcoming spirit.

Chapter 1

My Diary Entry

A miracle. What is it? Some describe it as a paranormal experience. Others as something unexplainable. An event brought about by magic or a supernatural being. In my profession, we call that being…God. The Bible also explains it as an unusual event caused by the power of God. For example, how after Lazarus being dead for four days, Jesus brought him back to life. Could you imagine sitting there with his sisters as he came walking out of the tomb? That's in John 11:33–44—a great story. What about the account in Matthew 14:13–21, where Jesus fed over five thousand people with only five loaves of bread and two fish and had leftovers. Now I know this was not my family. They leave no leftovers after meals. Reminds me of last Thanksgiving when Uncle Don—oh wait, I was making a point. God performed miracles back then and even now. They show who and what he is because only God can make things happen. Most of all, despite any circumstances we may face, he is sovereign and good. God is still in the miracle-working business today. I have seen him at work and do things that are not possible, and that was today.

I watched God use four people who barely knew each other before the day began. He brought them together and used them to heal others and themselves. All of them started the day with the same question: Why, God? This is Christmas Eve—well, Christmas Day. It is 4:41 a.m. as I enter this into my journal. This is not your typical holiday story but a life lesson on whom we should depend on and put our hopes into. We can lose sight of what is important—our surroundings make sure of that. But how do you get back up after you feel that life has flattened you and God has left the building? This is a story about tonight's occurrence when God moved into the lives of a deliveryman and his family. A traveling salesman many miles away from his family. A young businesswoman rising from the ashes of a lost loved one. And a jazz singer hiding from herself and the past. So before I get any further, I need to introduce myself.

My name is Reginald Jay Lamont, and that pastor I mentioned is me. Pastor Reggie, as the town, refers to me. I oversee the congregation at the church here in the town of Brentwood. Let me start by giving you a tour of our little city. Brentwood is between New York and Canada. It is about two hours away from Montreal and three hours from Vermont by car. We are so close to both that the United States and Canada can't decide to whom we belong, so neither claims us. I walk out to my front lawn, and I am in America, and my back driveway is in Canada. The city has a population of about two thousand. We have people from all colors and creeds and religions too, but we all seem to function fine. We are very current for a little city. We have the same stores, restaurants, and shops as most cities, but we have our own homegrown favorites. For example, people come from miles around to get Robin Bird's barbecue brisket and bacon. That tender, juicy, fall-apart, well-seasoned beef. Dripping with the sauce, melting in your mouth or that crispy all meat, little fat, thick-cut bacon strips. They are more like wedges. When the pro hockey team from Philadelphia goes to Winnipeg, their team bus sits right in front of the store. I made myself hungry—my apologies, I must focus.

Now where was I again? Oh right, our stores. The next big attraction is Pop's Place between Paul Street and Jenny Avenue near the mall. And yes, we have a mall with retail stores and a food gallery, even have an arcade/ laser tag place. How is that for an upscale mini city? (Hahaha!) But the best thing is it has a huge finished wood floor area in the middle of the mall for concerts and shows. We use it for events for the church, like tonight's Christmas service. But I will refer back to tonight's service later and talk about Pop's Place.

It is a family-owned tavern and has been around for thirty years by Harry Renfro. He was an ex-professional wrestler that went by the name of Deacon of Danger. His daughter now manages it and changed it into more of a family restaurant. It is the hip spot to go in this town. The best thing about the place is he made sure Jesus was discussed there, and everyone knew about it. He passed Jesus and the business on to his daughter, and she still owns it today. In fact, an enormous part of what went on tonight happened at Pop's. As for the biggest attraction is the best delivery and courier services on the planet. Funny thing, it is not mentioned along with the other top three services you could use, but everyone knows about them. Numbers do not lie. Whole Armor Delivery is the fastest, most efficient, and safest delivery company. I still can't figure out how they do it, and "amazing" does not do it enough justice. It is the warehouse about a block away from the church. It is a nice size, but you would not think it could even hold the business it does, but hey, who am I to say what can and can't be done? With God, all things are possible. I had to add that here, by law pastors must, it is like an unwritten rule. Because of the church members coming together, Brentwood became a town. Quakers and settlers from the west and then whoever wanted to worship and live God's way.

As the town grew, we grew, and God has raised pastors to deliver his Word. One being my great-uncle Melvin and the other uncle Rod (Rodney). Melvin the Great, as I called him, pastored here for fifty years, always talking Jesus, Jesus, Jesus. He never took credit for anything. God was always the answer. He would tell me, "Boy…if God ain't in it, you won't win it." For the longest time, I thought he meant me playing sports, but over time, it was a life-changing message. Uncle Rod came here to join him about thirty years ago from a small church in Detroit. He was the pastor there and came here to be Melvin the Great's assistant pastor and then a few years later a copastor. The first time I remember hearing my uncle mention ministry was Thanksgiving when I was eight.

It was late afternoon, and Mom finished putting the food on the table. I had been waiting all day for that turkey and stuffing. Quana could cook. Oh yeah, Quana is my lovely mother's name, and she could burn in the kitchen. Anyway, after everyone arrived at the house, Uncle Rod and Melvin were late as usual. We were ready to eat. As we gathered around the table, Mom spoke. I must admit I did not catch the first part of her speech because my stomach was talking louder than she was. She said she loved everyone, and she finished her talk. I did not realize what I was thinking fell out of my brain and then my mouth. Because I said "Finally!" loud enough for everyone to hear. My family laughed, and Mom looked down at me, smiled, and told me to hush. "Boy, we will eat soon." She wanted to thank the Lord for his provisions and the meal, so she asked Uncle Rod to pray over the food. Uncle Rod's prayers for grace could take hours, but today, something was out of the ordinary. Uncle Rod agreed and asked everyone to bow their heads. He cleared his throat as if he would begin and then silence. Rod then lifted his head and turned to Uncle Melvin. He said he thought the honor should go to the senior pastor.

Uncle Melvin, now looking surprised, asked, "Really?" He thanked his brother but declined because he thought Rod was the better choice. Uncle Rod disagreed because Melvin does the best prayers for the table. Uncle Melvin says Rod's prayers are more anointed, and the two go back-and-forth, trading compliments. I could not take it anymore; my stomach was roaring like an angry lion, and the food was getting cold. "Before Jesus comes back, can somebody pray?" is what I said, and how I am still alive is beyond me. The room became dead silent and if you could have seen my mother's face. I watched what seemed to be slow motion as her eyebrows bent, and her mouth contorted to a hard frown. Mom was mad and embarrassed. She scolded me about knowing better and to apologize to both of my uncles right now! Then something unexpected happened. My uncle Melvin interrupted Mom getting on my case. He told her I was right. Me, I was right? He then explained his position. He said we need not debate who does it but thank God for His blessings, and the best pastor in the room should do the prayer. Uncle Melvin then turns to me and tells me to bless the food.

Except for Rod and Melvin, everyone else was shocked. I did not believe it myself, so I verified it by asking if he was referring to me. If that was not shocking enough, he went further by saying, "Yes, you, Pastor, get with it. The food is getting cold."

I looked at my mom and saw the joy on her face. She even shed a tear or two. I did not know what to say. I spoke what was on my heart and rushed out an "Amen" at the end. Uncle Melvin took me to the side and told me something that I must admit was confusing yet familiar. He asked me if I had been dreaming a lot lately and to act on my ideas. I asked him why. I was honest because I had been, but I wanted to know how he knew and why it was happening. Uncle Melvin told me God had a plan for me and was preparing me for the future. Now to a kid, that was quite a lot to take in yet even understand. But he was right because, years later, these same ideas and dreams help me build programs at the church now. During his time in office, Melvin the Great was getting older and weaker, and Uncle Rod had to take over the helm. It was at his funeral when Uncle Rod told me he was now the pastor of the church. He also showed me a letter that Melvin the Great wrote three years before he got sick.

In the letter, he instructed Uncle Rod to call me in as his assistant. He said he had watched as God was preparing me for his works and the place I needed to be. And he believed it so much that he also left a package for me. For you to understand the significance of this, I must sidebar for a moment. Melvin the Great had this robe he would wear every Sunday. Your basic black robe, nothing special, but it had a beautiful clergy stole—I mean sharp. It was black and royal purple with gold sewn seams that look like little gold ropes at the bottom of each side and a gold cross and crown on each side and Jesus embroidered on the back of the yoke in gold—magnificent. When they prepared the body, they put him in his robe and stole for the burial. I guess I did not pay much attention when I did the eulogy. But the day after the funeral, we met at his house, and he showed me the letter and the package.

Uncle Rod says to me before he gives me the package that they both knew I was to be the pastor of this church, and yes, I denied it. Are you kidding? Not me! But what I did not tell him was I had been hearing God call me to ministry. I was not ready to accept it. Honestly, it scared me. Uncle Rod smiled and said to pray about it and open it when I get home. On my flight back to Delaware, I opened the package and wept in my seat. It was a good thing it was only five passengers that day. Inside the package was Melvin the Great's stole and a note from Uncle Rod. He was told to give it to me because I would need it. When I did finally return home between the rides from the airport to the house, I had time to have it float in my mind. I found myself angry, and I guess, betrayed. How dare they make plans and not tell me—*me*! I am the one you are dropping your business on. You two know nothing about what plans I have. Don't add me to whatever is going on over there. I don't know those people. I thought my anger was at my uncles' expense for both, but I got checked by God that night. I prayed before I went to bed, as always. But it was more of me saying what I was not ready for. Telling God in a way he was making a mistake telling them (if he did, not sure), I was ready and to move out there—*please*! I kind of had to laugh a bit before the sheets even fell on my body. It was off to sleep I go (11:00 p.m.). Off to sleep (12:02 a.m.). Going to sleep now (1:05 a.m.). Sleep I go (2:20 a.m.).

Okay, you get the picture. No rest that night. I gave up, got out of bed, and went to the kitchen. I needed to go shopping, but for now, Aunt Rhoda's apple pie will do, and look, eggnog ice cream. Yes, sir, we can salvage the night. I grabbed the mail that I had not read while I was away. And yes, I put the whole pint of ice cream on the whole apple pie and went to my desk. The first thing I opened was a parcel envelope from Mom. I love my mom. Each month, she sends a monthly devotional book she gets from her church. That woman prayed and made sure we knew God for ourselves and still does. I opened it to find I was a day behind already, so since I was up, I will read both. I was not ready for what was about to come. If you ask God to speak or he has something to tell you, he uses his Word.

The first devotional was from Exodus 3:11–22 when God called Moses. He told Moses to leave and get his people from Egypt. Moses asked God who should he tell Pharaoh who sent him. In his mind, he was not ready for such a task. God told him he was with him and instructed him to have faith. Then Moses was to tell the people their God has sent him to them. But Moses with doubt, a bit of sarcasm, and fear asked God, "Who shall I say sent me?" At that point, God tells Moses exactly who and what he is. I am sure it made

Moses jump out of his robe, but at that moment, I felt the fear. At that exact time, he was no longer talking to Moses—he was talking to me. He used my full name. I went to my Heavenly Father like some mixed-up teenager about what I would not do. But as a great parent would do, he put me in my place and made his directions clear. As I looked up from the little book, I had set on my Bible, I could see on my couch was the package that had my uncle's stole in it. It was hanging out of the package. I don't remember a lot about that night because I woke up on the couch. The stole was out of the package and on the chair in front of me, and my hand was in a pan of melted ice cream and crust chunks. But I called my uncle Rod that afternoon, and we talked for hours. A month after that conversation, I was shipping my stuff and me to Brentwood. So here we are, four years later. I spent two in seminary school, a year as an associate pastor to Uncle, and now pastor. Things have been good over the time I spent here. I started some new programs while updating others. We will expand the church next year, adding a gym, kitchen, and classroom space. Things are well, but I must be honest, there are some things that are not what or where I expected. But this year, it is not only me feeling this way.

Chapter 2

The Businesswoman

I have to give Harriet her due for making Pop's Place what it is today. The former bar now turned sports-themed restaurant was all her work. I am so glad her father got to see it before he passed. Those two were very close, almost like best friends. I miss the big guy, and lately, I see the loss in her eyes. This was her dad's time of year. He loved Christmas and passed that same love of the holiday on to Harriet. Oh, how we loved the stories he would tell.

You would never think this gorgeous woman, who looked like a runway model, was a tree-swinging, car-loving tomboy. Her father raised Harriet as a single parent. He came off the road and gave up his wrestling career to do it. He signed with the big wrestling promotion in Connecticut too. Never got details on her mom or what happened to her, and Harriet didn't remember. But no matter what he did to raise her as a young woman, Harriet loved sports and her cars. Henry had the help of the church moms, and even his sister Ressa stayed with them to help raise her. After services, you could find her in the tree behind Donnie's Tire Shop or running over two boys scoring a touchdown. Even today, she is still a tough little egg, but in church, a Jesus sponge. There was nothing that would stop her from learning about God. Harry loved the Lord. He taught his daughter about having a personal relationship with God. When Harry sat with people, young and old, he would tell his stories about his wrestling career. Men, children, and yes, even women would come to hear his stories. There would be Harriet, listening and enjoying with the rest of us, about Harry going through each battle and struggle. I have to say the one thing that has stuck with me, even now, is he would say, "I have battled the biggest and the baddest, carried men on my back to win world titles in many countries. But none of that compares to the men and women's lives saved by Jesus carrying them on his back as he carried that cross to Calvary." How awesome is that? I miss you, Harry.

Well, anyway, Harriet grew up over the years and has grown to be a beautiful woman of God—heck woman, period. She went to the local high school and graduated at the top of her class. They offered her scholarships from some top colleges in the United States and Canada. Harriet could have gone on a scholarship for basketball or volleyball but chose the business scholarship with the idea in mind to help her father increase his business. And that she did. After she graduated, she came back to town with a plan and a legacy for her father in mind. In less than six months, she convinced her dad to make the changes and not miss a day of business during the renovation. Pops went from just being the local tavern to the family restaurant you see today. That also reminds me about the time Harriet paid off her dad's mortgage for the restaurant, about three years ago, as a Christmas gift. He praised Jesus during the whole service that Sunday after, but he was more thankful for the blessing of his daughter.

But let me get back on track here. The Renfros loved Christmas and celebrating the gift of Jesus to the world but also the joy of being a kid waiting for Santa. When she was younger, Harriet and her dad would prepare the milk and cookies for Santa. Then Harry would sneak downstairs to put together the racetracks and sporting goods until early in the morning. What an awesome time to be a child and a parent during the holidays.

Even as Harriet got older, they still celebrated with the same joy and love and became each other's Santa, but you would never know the difference. About two years ago, Harry's back bothered him. We thought it was an old wrestling injury. He was lifting a few cases of soda and pulled his back at the restaurant. He had a slipped disk, and after the operation, it fused back into place. Harry was tough! After a few months of rest, he was right back behind the bar, serving drinks and welcoming customers. What no one knew was that he had an infection in his back and when diagnosed, it was too late, and Harry died. That was last year, a week before Christmas. Harriet still honored Christmas for her father, decorating and helping to keep spirits up, but I still worry for her. She hadn't had time to mourn her dad, and that worried me. Yes, we knew he was in heaven and no worries or pain. But this was her father. She buried herself in her work and helped at church, but Harriet had no time to deal with her own problems. From time to time, she had that same look in her eyes as she had at the funeral. When she asked me, "What do I do now?" and for the first time, I had to tell her I did not know.

Chapter 3

The Diva

Next, we have Williamena Lorraine Davis or, as we know her around town, Billie or the Drunk Diva. Now I know what you are thinking. "Pastor, how could you say that about someone? Aren't you about saving people? Where are those gifts of love and forgiveness?" So let me answer your questions. Jesus saves, not me! I plant the seeds. He waters and cares for the garden. I speak the truth, so what I say is not a lie! The woman is a trip. But most of all, I keep Billie in prayer daily. Things are going on with her that she needs to work on with Jesus. Billie has been in this town for about five years now ever since she skipped out on that promoter and his jazz concert. Must have been some big money for her to leave Nashville, Tennessee! I guess the bottle can do that when you lose faith in God and yourself. Wait, I may have lost you, so let me explain.

Billie went by the stage name of Amber Naomi. You remember, the jazz/R&B vocalist who performed with almost every artist possible? From Old Blue Eyes to the King of Pop, Billie performed with them all. She won many awards, including five Grammy Awards. Well-traveled and known, Billie spent years across the music charts. She traveled the world with her soulful voice. At some point, the lifestyle she gained meant more than her music. Her concerts were questionable, and that was if she even performed. But at the after-parties, planned or not, Billie performed. The more she drank, the more she became as we now know her, the Drunk Diva.

So as time has gone by and the other generations of singers have come through, Billie became obsolete. She tried to push her former status over the years to get work, but it's her Drunk Diva status that people seem to remember. She cleaned up her act a few years ago, sought help for the drinking, and even got a spot on the Legends of Jazz tour. During the tour, Drunk Diva returned. She owed money for not appearing, and Amber Naomi disappeared. Billie has been here with us, making her home/office over at Pop's Place. She was a psychiatrist, town news reporter, relationship guru, and self-appointed copastor of every church or worship center. How Harriet dealt with her daily showed me there were angels here on earth. She seemed to have kept Billie under control over the years. But don't let it fool you. Billie knew how to get to Harriet. It was Harriet's dad that was a big fan of hers and allowed her to hang around the place. On the jukebox inside Pops are three of her top hits. So I guess you can say he left her as an inheritance to Harriet when he passed. Her father talked to Billie daily about life with Jesus and how he can change your life, and Harriet has continued to do the same. From time to time, when she felt Billie was open, Harriet would invite me to lunch to talk to her about Christ. But like the journalist she was, there were people in this town that think Harriet and I were dating. Now before you say anything, Harriet and I are wonderful friends and nothing more. She is a great woman of God, a talented business-woman, and has what I think is the prettiest smile and disposition. We both liked sports and watch wrestling. Did I mention her bacon and lettuce and tomato club sandwiches? They are off the hook.

Anyway, back to Billie, as much as we try, she would not go to church. There were some hurts there too, but we as the body of Christ must stop judging and help more. So that was why I didn't give up on Billie and did what I could. Harriet thought it would be a good idea for Billie to help with the Toy Drive this year. So a few hours before the Christmas service, she would pick up and wrap the gifts to give out. Little did she know it would have her at service tonight. Yes, I know that was sneaky, but sometimes you gotta be creative. It was Harriet's idea, not mine. I wish I could take the credit.

Chapter 4

The Salesman

The four people I mentioned are all from our town, except one. He is from Portland, Oregon, USA. Mr. David Samport. David is the business manager and sales director of Bossk Beverages, the largest flavored water distributor in the states, looking to do business in Canada. David married his high school sweetheart, Sarah, and they have two children—Davey, twelve, and Rhonda, nine. Life has not been easy. They started with love and hard work. But the thing David attributes to his success is his wife's faith in Jesus. This helped him to find God for himself. And through prayer, worship, he watched his faith grow, and God's blessings fall upon them. So saying Christmas is their favorite time of year would be a bit of an understatement. The Samport Christmas would be something you would see in a movie. Worship, church, family, and food—awesome! David even takes off the entire week to enjoy the time with his family. So why is he in Canada on Christmas Eve?

Here's the thing. David was stuck here in Canada, and he had to explain it to his family. So let's go back a month for some background on his story. David and Sarah planned something different this year. They would celebrate Christmas at home, as always. But the day after, the family would go to Sarah's mom and dad's house, staying with them for two days after the New Year. David would leave from there the day after New Year to attend a one-day business lecture at his college before returning home. Everything was set, tickets purchased, plans made, family members notified. It was to be great. Three days before Christmas Eve, David gets "the call" that Bossk

Beverages has been waiting for—Clermont Drinks and Beverages. The biggest distributor in Canada wanted to discuss carrying David's products. This was huge! Bossk would go from being one of the largest distributors in the United States to becoming the second largest in North America. He thought, *Merry Christmas to us! Hallelujah! Thank you, Jesus!* But sometimes we must make sure it is God that is doing the blessing and not us. Even if it meant more money for the company, it also meant more time away from his family.

Sarah explained her displeasure of the disruption of going on Christmas Eve. "Why do or must we meet at 10:00 a.m. on Christmas Eve? Why so soon? It can't wait till after the holidays? Why don't you come here? What do I tell the family if something happens? Most of all, we have not even prayed about this. It makes no sense." It bothered David for a moment, but he saw the fear and hurt in her eyes, so he sat her down to talk. He assured her it would not affect their plans. He promised everything would be good. He would fly in that morning, go to the meeting at ten, the meeting would be over by one o'clock. He would then go to the airport to catch his two-thirty flight and back home by six in time for church. How he got her to go for it, I will never know, but he convinced the kids and in-laws. Hey, he is a salesman by trade.

So it was Christmas Eve, and David was in his meeting. It went well. All parties left happy with each other. They did not realize the meeting went over by two hours and twenty minutes—in case you are not keeping count. That puts the time at 2:20 p.m. Time to get to the airport—twenty minutes. The flight is at two thirty. It hit David like a bag of bricks. He tried to call the airport but could not get through. The president of Clearvoyant offered his limousine to get him to the airport. But when he arrived, his flight was gone. David even tried to bargain for another flight leaving that day.

"I will take anything," he begged, but the next flight home was 3:30 p.m., the day after Christmas. But the only thing he could book for that day was a room at the bed-and-breakfast outside of our town. His demeanor mirrored that the phone call home had not gone well at all. Disappointed kids and in-laws, a hurt, upset, and teary-eyed wife—not good. I am sure he heard "I told you so" many times. After the call, he was in his room for a few hours alone. First, remorseful, then angry, and shortly after, mourning. It was a major pity party, and you would think for himself. Unfortunately, it was for God. How could you let this happen? Why give me something that could cause so much harm? It was horrible. I think God was sitting there, saying, "When did you bother to discuss this with me, let alone wreck what I put together, silly child of mine?"

Feeling empty inside, David thought he would go out for a burger. He called a taxi and asked the driver for the best place to get one. That is how he ended up at Pop's Place. Well, that is what he thought, but there is nothing like being in a room full of people and feeling alone, especially when God wants your attention and has a plan for you. It is here where he met the other people in this story and a group of folks with the same Christmas spirit. He came in and was quiet—well, at first—but when Harriet tried to play some holiday music, the place was not in agreement. No one there really wanted to hear the joyful tunes coming from the jukebox. David joined with the negative talk of the others. But something inside Harriet let her know he was not like the rest. She felt it was more out of a loss than anything else. Something that Harriet knew first-hand, so she went to find out what his story was. But then the Diva stepped in and caused the entire place, including David, to become disarrayed. I don't think that woman is even five feet tall, but every inch, trouble—I'm sorry, *trouble*!

Chapter 5

The Delivery Guy

Now the ultimate piece and the most important part of the puzzle—the Kerfees family! Eric, the big guy with an enormous heart, lives in town with his wife, the lovely Selina, and their son Christopher. Eric owns and runs the Whole Armor Delivery Service. This company has been around for a long time. Passed down from generation to generation, father to son. The business does very well, especially during the holidays, and beats any postal or commercial delivery service year after year. The warehouse is on the border of the town, about five minutes from their home. Eric and Selina's son Chris is thirty-five years old, married to Denise Pettaway, a young lady he met here at the church. And they have two kids Tara and Justice who call Eric their "Big Paw." Eric is a kind and influential man of God. He made sure his family was in church every Sunday for worship. His first ministry was always his family. And he made sure they took part in ministries and functions. For years, he and Harriet's dad led the men's ministry. They helped my uncle and I tutor, mentor, and befriend many of our brothers in town and out. It's funny how as men we find it so hard to express ourselves and keep so much in till we blow up or stress out. But these guys made it easy to talk and relate to life and daily trials as men.

Harry and Eric also ran the outreach ministry to help less fortunate families, making sure they met their needs as best as possible. This was their best time of year—collecting toys and goods, handing them out after our Christmas Eve service and program. They made sure it was very festive and spent four months planning it alone. One year, about twenty years ago, Eric showed up in a Santa Claus suit riding on a sleigh he built in his shed from a lawn mower and started handing out the gifts after service. To say that was the most memorable year is an understatement. Funny, but no one ever noticed that Eric resembled Santa, except at the time his beard was white with some black and a hint of gray but now all white. Eric had been doing it ever since that day, and after each Eve service, everyone looked forward to seeing him.

Eric was getting older and looking to retire. He and Selina were looking forward to traveling and spending more time together. He did not say much about it, but over the years, you could see that he was getting tired. I know he wanted to pass the business on to Chris, as his father did for him. That was not what Chris had in mind because no matter what he did, it was not a fit for him. Chris majored in accounting, so he did well with the books for his father. The whole idea of delivery and shipping orders was just not his thing. Chris always liked the missions' field going out to help people while he spread the Word of God. I have spoken to Chris about his desire. He had even helped us establish contact with a small mission group the church now supports. He wanted to tell his dad but did not want to disappoint him. In the middle of all this was Selina. More than being a great homemaker, she did wonders here at the church for the women's ministry. She sounded like an angel in the choir. If you close your eyes, you might think the roof opens and the songs come straight from heaven. Last year, because of her solo, we were asked to be part of a choir competition in California. We did not make it, but it was a nice invitation. Anyway, Selina got to hear it from both sides and in her way mediates between the two. Eric and Chris both told her their plans and problems with each other. She tried to keep both on an even level, but she knew they needed to talk to each other. This past summer, she decided enough was enough and put them on a crash course meeting with destiny. And it would catch them both by surprise.

Chapter 6

The Summer of Reveal

It was mid-July when Selina received a call at the house from an excited Chris and Denise. He reminded her of their conversation when he told her about the work he was doing at his new church home. Chris informed her he received the blessing of a new job. Selina was happy to hear her son was happy and found a job that would supply and support his little family. Not to confuse you, but a bit of back information will help make sense of this and tie things together. Three years ago, Chris took an accountant job at New Faith Church, which is about two hours away from our church. He attended their Bible study after work and talked with the pastor about his thoughts about missions. Shortly after taking Denise to visit the church, they started attending New Faith. Now I was not happy to have them go. But when God calls you and there is peace in the decision, follow God. They have been members there for about two years now and helped build a mission's ministry. It began to grow quite large in that time: six countries, twelve active missionaries, all through Chris and Denise's faithfulness and vision from God—awesome! I hear you asking, "So where are you going with this?"

Well, Chris was promoted to missionary ministering director for New Faith Church. He would be the leader of the entire program by going out to help and visit the missionaries abroad. So now he had two jobs through the church, one as the director and the other as an independent accountant. Chris would move to Yvonneville, so they would leave our town. Selina and Eric might not like that a lot, but they understood what comes with growth. While Chris was explaining the job to Selina, she had a moment of recall and sadness that she hid from him. Two days ago, she surprised Eric at the warehouse and took him to lunch. A surprise was definitely there, but more for Selina than Eric. A construction crew working inside added two new offices and larger shelves near the shipping dock. It surprised Eric that she was there, but he was happy that he could finally tell her the plans he had for the business. As he showed her all the adjustments to the building, she noticed the biggest change was Chris's name on the door to the biggest office with the title CEO/manager. She was remembering how happy she was to see her son's name and to hear about her husband's plans for Chris.

As she came out of her recollection, still on the phone, she realized how much her son had no interest in the business. Chris does the accounting for the company but just to be a help to his dad. Chris told his mom how his dream was to be in missions. With him now being the missionary director, part of the job is to visit and help the missionaries abroad. So for the next two years, he, Denise, and the girls would travel to other countries. Selina felt her heart sink to her feet, and Chris could hear it in her voice. She was a mother, and her emotions spilled out, and she had every right, and Chris understood. She also had to deal with this information, knowing about all the changes Eric was making for Chris without telling him. She also realized that God was present and blessing, but it still did not make things any easier.

She told Chris her concerns but knew that God will take care of it all. She needed time for it to sink in. She asked Chris when he would tell his father, and like Eric, he said soon, unless she would tell Dad for him. Selina, being a wise woman of God and knowing this needed to be discussed sooner than later, told Chris to bring the family over for a barbecue this Saturday at one o'clock and have Denise make the potato salad and her famous two-layer cheesecake. She and Chris ended the call, and she continued to plan. She told Eric to only work until two thirty on Saturday because the kids are coming for dinner. So as she planned, the kids showed at one o'clock and helped set up for dinner. Chris got the grill up and going and the tables up, not knowing he was being set up by his mother. She sent Chris to the warehouse to go get his father and bring him home to cook and play with the grandkids. It was earlier than planned, but Chris drove over to the warehouse and all looked the same. The ride down the hill, past the lake, in the parking lot, and past the gate to the back-service door. It was all the same as any other time until he walked into the work area. There he saw all the recent construction and the added office space.

Eric came from the back talking to one of the construction workers signing papers on a clipboard. It surprised him that his son was there early, but even more to see the questionable look on Chris's face. Now rushing the worker away, Eric went to address Chris. He hugged his boy and asked him what he was doing here so early as he moved to block a certain office door. They banter back and forth about the business and the changes made to the warehouse. Chris lets Eric know that Mom told him he has been spending more time there, and now he could see why. Chris told his father he loved the changes. It looked as if he made his workload easier, especially with the holidays only months away. Eric was so glad to hear his son's approval of the workshop and told him again the story of the family business—how it passed down from father to son. Chris interrupted, not to be rude to him but to save him time from telling the story he heard hundreds of times. Eric got the message and smiled as he got down to the point he was making to his son. Eric lets Chris know he is handing over the business to him, pulling the cover off the name-plate on the door he was trying to hide. He was now the president and CEO of the delivery business, and Chris could not hide his facial expression of surprise and remorse.

Chris spoke, "No, Pop, I can't—"

But Eric interrupted with "Believe it? I know, but it is true, and you can start training."

With a deeper voice and conviction, Chris tells his dad, "No, I can't, and I mean I cannot."

Confused, Eric asked his boy for an explanation of what he was trying to say. This was not going how he thought. Chris explained the details of his life goal as he did to his mother on the phone. As each detail rolled from his lips, you could see Eric's heart ran up to his throat and back down to the pit of his stomach. When hurt and disappointment come together, they can meld into a nice mass of anger. You could see the transformation as Eric sat down in his reclining desk chair. With now his hands folded in front of his face, he cut into the information given.

"So let me get this straight. You are taking my grandkids away. And you and the family are going to leave the country for a year, in a few months no less! But you won't work one job, the family business, and not have to uproot your family. That makes no sense to me, Christopher Jason!"

Chris interrupted his tirade and responded in a forceful way Eric did not expect, "It was you who told me to follow the Word of Christ and his Word for the will of my life. Every day, you would say, 'As for me and my house, we will follow the Lord.' You made sure we were under the Word and in church every Sunday…Bible study on Thursday. You know what, I thought you would be happy for what is being done in your son's life."

Although Chris was making excellent points, he did not care for his tone. Eric got up from his chair and made it known he was still the father and warned him to not cross the respect line. Chris apologized to his father and let him know he was not trying to upset him, how he loved and respected him as a dad and a hero. He tried to follow in Eric's footsteps, and it was not working for either of them. Eric finally had to admit to his son and himself that he agreed with him. God had another plan for Chris, and he finally received the plan and everything he wanted and prayed for. Eric finally, with relief and remorse, told his boy about how he could never get Chris to clean his room, but he listened to him now. He also let him know how proud of him and how much he loved him. Chris expressed his love for his father and wanted to drive him back to the house for the family dinner. Eric sent Chris ahead and let him know to let the grandkids know he was coming to start the biggest water balloon fight ever. After Chris left the office, Eric sat back down in his chair with a slight smile and a brief chuckle. He was thinking how he was blessed and how God blessed his family, but then reality washed over him like a wave, and now he was left with the thought, *What do I do now?*

Chapter 7

Christmastime Is Here

It is December 24. You know, the day before Christmas. The holiday spirit is falling by the side of the road for a few folks around the town, including me. I know the Lord will provide and he has everything, but I have my human times. We have a Christmas program tonight and not even enough gifts to cover the kids in the town. We have half as many gifts as last year, and the food donations are nowhere close to feeding the guests. It is so low we are going out collecting donations today. I had to make an emergency plea to the congregation and town this past Tuesday. I did not want to do it and was ready to cancel the program this year. God has been pressing me to continue. So out I go with Tina, our family service director for the church, and of all people, Billie. Eric, after a heavy night at the warehouse, kicks the snow off his boots before he enters the back door of his home. He hung up his coat on a hook by the door and grabbed a bottle of water before he sat down at his kitchen table.

It was full of bills, schedules, and assorted other paperwork waiting for him to review. Eric looks over the table and sighs. He then goes into his back pocket to pull out a brochure. It is for a holiday cruise to the Caribbean, seven days of relaxation and fun. A smile crossed his face as he thought about the warm breeze, the food, the view. Then his look turned into frustration and then sadness as he leaned back in his chair. Eric took a deep sigh and had a brief discussion with his Heavenly Father. He let him know he knew God would never put more on him than he could bear. Eric did not know how much more he could take. He expressed his need for a long vacation.

From the other room, his best friend and wife, Selina, called out, making sure it was him in the kitchen. She came in to greet him with a kiss on the forehead, as she always does when he gets home, and asked him how his day was going.

Unlike any other day, Eric did not respond instead sighed and pushed some papers on the table over to the side to look at others. When he finally spoke, he let her know about the weekly schedule and how much work needs to get done. He picked up several envelopes only to find no holiday greeting cards but bills. Now frustrated, Eric lashed out about the bills, questioning if they were new and how he paid them. Selina, in her calm, loving voice, reminded him he paid the bills…last month. She brought him back down with her calming voice, and he apologized for his tone. Eric explained to his wife that his disposition over the bills and schedules was the reason he wanted to take a holiday vacation this week. Time was flying by, and he could not seem to get a break anywhere. He needed a vacation, and if Chris took over the business, he could have done that. Selina listened to her husband but interrupted him with a sad dose of reality. She explained how the trip was not possible this time of year. The kids love seeing him at the mall and when they receive their gifts from the church after the Christmas Eve service, not to mention his very own grandkids would miss seeing their Big Paw at Christmas.

She expressed to him he still has not accepted Chris's decision not to go into the business. She had to remind him he was not cut out to follow him into the business. He is taking care of his wife and kids with the two jobs, and they are happy. Eric then tried to explain his side as if he was in court in front of a judge. If he came into the business, he would only need one job, he would have been a manager, and not have to move his family. Instead, he would rather be all over the place, not knowing what will happen. And they will bring the toys for his kids, but they don't mind because they are the grands. Eric stopped himself and took a deep breath and sighed. He thought this was the worst time of the year, but even worse, he did not realize he had also verbalized his thought. Hearing this Selina, yet stern, reminded Eric how he used to love this time of year and what it stood for. What she said hit a nerve with him. He let her know that things have changed; the world has changed. How people have forgotten what this time of year is all about. Selina was now upset herself but, still trying to keep the situation civil, told Eric that he could not forget what this was all about because God had not forgotten him.

She told him, "Woe is me never looked good on him, so why wear it now like a Sunday morning suit?"

Eric jumped up out of his seat, grabbed his coat and car keys off their respective hooks, and headed out the kitchen back door. Following him, Selina asked Eric where he was going and reached for his arm. Eric stopped and addressed her about going to the mall to play Stupid Claus for all the good little girls and boys. Eric pulled away and continued with his exit. He was mumbling under his breath, unhappy with his wife's words as he walked toward the car. He reached down to grab the door handle and stopped himself. He thought why did he feel alone in this. No one seemed to care about this holiday, its meaning, or for him. Looking to the sky, he asked the Lord why he has been forsaken and what the purpose was for it. Eric turned from the car and walked down the hill to the town shopping center and a small group of businesses.

Chapter 8

Pop's Place

As Eric walked down the hill, his heart spoke to him, and he felt remorse. He knew his wife was trying to console and be honest with him. Eric decided that as soon as he got back home, he'd apologize to her, but for now, he needed some time to himself. And the best way to do that was in a corner booth with some spicy wings at Pop's. Harriet and David were still discussing his situation. He told her how he dreaded calling his wife and telling her what was happening, especially since she was against him going. Harriet agreed he was not in the best position and allowed David to continue. "I was trying to improve our lives," he said. His wife, Sarah, told him they did not pray about it or even ask God if this was for them. He jumped at the opportunity. Harriet, who had been very attentive listening until then, had to speak. She did not want to add fuel to the fire of David's guilt. She let him know that not talking to God before making choices is never good. David, now because of this, would miss Christmas with his family. Harriet, still wanting to be optimistic, tried to make David feel better and came up with an idea.

Yes, he would miss Christmas day, but he could still go home to be with them the day after. David informed her of the total plans the family had for the holidays. They were planning to fly out the day after to stay with his wife's family until New Year. Also, David was flying out the same day to a business conference and won't see the family until three days later. Harriet apologized and was sad for David's dilemma. He agreed and accepted the condolence. Harriet is a fighter and would not allow joy to leave her or anyone in her presence. With a smile, Harriet said he needed a good dose of her father's famous feel-better tonic. David was now curious and asked her exactly what that was.

With a huge smile, she said, "A Redemption Slam," and made her way to the other side of the counter. A minute or two later, she returned with a tall metal tumbler and two glasses. David asked her what this was again before she poured it into the cups. Harriet laughed and told him the name was Redemption Slam, otherwise known as a strawberry milkshake. For the first time, David smiled. After his first sip, his smile grew even larger, even with a slight giggle. Harriet asked what was so funny. So at first, David said nothing but then told her what was going on in his head. Strawberry was his favorite flavor for a milkshake. And that the name of her milkshake was very familiar. He told her when he was younger, he and his dad would get shakes. After they went to wrestling matches on Saturday afternoons, Redemption Slam was the name of his favorite wrestler's finishing move.

As if in disbelief, Harriet smiled and gasped, "Oh really?"

David then talked about the Deacon of Danger. For ten minutes, he went into his career, Southern Wrestling, his greatest opponents, and the titles he held. David was so in a zone of memories he even repeated one of his greatest speeches and said his catchphrase, "This ring is—"

Harriet interrupted and finished the statement with "Is my church."

Shocked, David agreed and asked if she was a fan. "You could say that," Harriet agreed now, trying to hide her smile.

Billie, who had been eavesdropping at her table, told David that the Deacon of Danger was Harriet's daddy. Harriet nodded and went to the back counter. She opened a cabinet on the wall and pulled out a black canvas bag. Out of it comes a big gold championship belt and a photo of the two after he won the title. Harriet then confirmed the Deacon was her father, Harry Renfro. David looked as if he was a child holding his hero's achievement in his hands. The only word that came from him was "Wow!" He then finally introduced himself. Realizing he never told her his name or even who he was addressing, this was the Deacon's daughter. Harriet then told him her name and that she owned the tavern he was in. David thanked her for the hospitality and for sharing history with him. David thought it would be great to meet the man he watched every Saturday with his father. He asked Harriet would it be possible to see her father in person, for a photo, something to show his dad.

Harriet informed David that Harry passed a few weeks before Christmas last year. After seeing her face change, he apologized and asked her how she was holding up. It could not be easy for her or her family during the holidays. Harriet let him know she was okay. Her dad loved the holidays, and it helps to celebrate in his honor. Even with her mind on her father, she tried to lift David. She let him know her father loved his fans and would have taken that picture in a second. David asked if it was okay to find out what happened to the Deacon and how he passed. Harriet agreed and began with what happened a few years before his death. Harry was bringing up cases of beer from the basement and pulled a vertebra in his back and moved two disks. He was down for two weeks but ignoring the doctor's orders and went right back to work. David, confused, stated that that did not sound fatal, and Harriet agreed. Not at first, but over time, something they did not detect crept in. He caught a staph infection between the disk and bone, and it killed him.

David now fell into his feelings and apologized to Harriet. He did not want to bring up terrible memories for her and bring her down because he was. David apologized again. He felt like he was killing everyone around him during the holiday. Harriet, realizing his mood, let David know that he was not going to be sad and negative in her establishment. This was her father's favorite time, so she celebrates to remember him. David told her that now he understood why she was pushing for joy in the tavern. She added that and the birth of her Lord and Savior Jesus. David gave her a hearty amen and asked if he could answer a question that he had been holding on to for a few years now. Harriet agreed to do her best if she knew the answer. He asked her about her father's disappearance from the wrestling scene. He was to sign with a big company near Connecticut and was never heard from again.

Harriet told him she could answer the question. But before his funeral, she did not know the answer. Harriet then went into telling the story of the day of the funeral. As everyone was leaving, three wrestlers came to see her at the same time. What their names were, she did not recall because when she met them, she was young. Harriet remembers them as Uncles Ted, Dave, and Rich. She thanked them for coming and honoring her father with their words. They told her Harry was one of them and a friend—to one, he was even his trainer. They reminisce about how good of a man he was, how funny, and honorable. Harriet agreed to let them know it sounded exactly like her father. She began smiling at the splendid memories. They also wanted her to know how much he loved his daughter; Tater Tot is what he would call her. You could see her blushing as they mentioned her nickname without even hearing her say, "Oh, Dad." Harriet was then surprised when one wrestler stated. Now he could see why Harry never took the contract.

Puzzled, she turned to him and asked what contract he was referring to. He told her about the contract to wrestle for that big group in Connecticut. Then realized she did not know what her father had done. Another of the wrestlers explained to Harriet what she heard. "Harry, Ted, Dave, and Rich went to the corporate office to sign contracts to wrestle for the company. Each of us signed our contracts, and we all left together to celebrate making a big time. Two weeks later, when we were at our first show, Harry was nowhere, a no-show." Another of the wrestlers entered the conversation, letting her know that is when they found out he did not sign his contract. His reason—he did not want to leave her with her aunt. He wanted to make sure Harriett had one full-time parent in her life. That is why he turned down the contract and retired from the business. He did it with no remorse because he loved her more than his career.

Harriet questioned her father's decision not to tell her. Then her uncles surrounded and hugged her together to protect her and lift her up. David told Harriet he understood what her father did, and he would have done the same for his daughter. Harriet remembered he said he had kids and asked about his daughter. He told her his daughter's name was Rhonda, and his son was David Jr. or Davey.

He let her know he would miss them tomorrow. Harriet reassured David everything would be okay. God was still in the miracle-making business. David, now falling back into the feelings he came in with, disagreed, nodded, and slumped over his cup.

Eric finally reached the parking lot of the tavern. As he got closer, he could hear happy Christmas music playing. He also heard something else, people complaining. That was something never heard coming from Pop's, but he recognized the biggest voice there and the ringleader—Billie. Before going in, he peeked through the gigantic front window. He saw Billie inside, stirring up the trouble. Then he recognized a businessman whom he never saw before but felt like he knew and about five more patrons. As Eric listened, he found out that the loud discussion was over Harriet Renfro playing holiday music on the jukebox. Billie, tipsy with that raspy voice, was complaining, asking, "What is this? I came in here to get away from this, and why are we forced to have the holidays jammed down our throats?"

The businessman agreed with adding, "This is not the best time."

Seeing that David agreed with her, Billie thought she found a new friend. She went to cozy up to David and place her arm around him; Without even looking up, he politely removed her arm and moved his seat away from her.

Harriet, whom you could always find smiling and uplifting, turned to everyone there and gave them what was on her heart.

"It is Christmas, and I will not let your sad sacks steal my joy. My God can do above all that we can ask or think. So your situations, whatever they may be, are not as bad as they seem. This is the time of year for miracles."

Billie, not allowing anyone to have the last word in anything, tells her, "And Christmas miracles are like this time of year. Sad!"

Eric then watched as the businessman that was a few moments ago on Billie's side came to the defense of Harriet. This guy tells Billie not to be so hard on her and tells his story about how he loved the holiday too—being with family and friends, worshiping at service. He even laughed when he described the food. But then his face changed and was sad as he made the statement, "Everything must end at some point."

Harriet felt his pain, but unbeknownst to the group, so did Eric. Harriet asked why it ended. He was full of joy talking about it, and even Billie agreed and got quiet. It ended this year; he went to a conference for his company, and they extended the meeting for two hours. He had to cancel his flight home and book a later flight, only to find out his flight was the last one out for the day. The next flight is not scheduled to leave until the morning after Christmas. He would miss his family and the celebration. Harriet tried to assure him things would be okay. He would have to see them the day after. But then Eric heard one of the saddest things ever. The day after his wife and kids are flying out to see his wife's family and won't be back until the day after New Year's. He also had a conference planned that next day, so he could not meet them before they left. He said his wife is devastated, and when he spoke of his kids, he put his head down. Harriet, now sad herself, expressed how sorry she was and did not know how severe it was. He said thanks and shrugged his shoulders, his head dropping more. Even Billie came over and put her arm around him and shared a consoling word. Or so they thought. Billie was eight when she first saw the transgression. She would watch her mom sneak downstairs, always around 12:15 a.m. and 12:30 a.m., and meet that man named Santa Claus. He had a fake beard and a pillow hanging out under his big coat, looking sloppy. You could see her getting upset as she told them.

Her poor daddy was upstairs sleeping. Momma would be all over him, kissing and hugging. Oh, that man, that man, how she hated that man! She could not stand that man! Billie then turned away from the group as if she would cry. David, who is a businessman, thought her story sounded very familiar. Harriet was thinking the same, and knowing Billie, she would understand it. Then Harriet heard the song playing on the jukebox. That old Christmas song about seeing "Mommy Kissing Santa Claus." Now Harriet knew Billie was up to something. She asked what was so traumatic about that. Billie broke out in a big belly laugh and told Harriet she got her!

"My family never celebrated Christmas. We were Jewish and sang, 'Dreidel... Dreidel... Dreidel, I made you out of clay.'"

Now trying not to laugh with her, Harriet scolded Billie about lying in her place. Billie, still laughing, told Harriet that she was no fun and how she needed something. Harriet, knowing what would come from Billie's mouth, cut her off. Then Billie saw the pastor coming down the street. She remembered that she promised to help him with the toy drive, and she was late. As she got to the door, she let Harriet know she needed a man and ran out the door. She almost knocked Eric down as she scurried up the street.

Chapter 9

The Attitude Maker

In rushing out, the door made snowfall off the awning and on Eric's head. It was not a big deal, but now it put him in a really foul mood. He thought how rude Billie was and how his neck was now cold and wet. Eric went into the tavern, and instead of finding his favorite booth, he found a seat at the end of the counter. Harriet did not notice him come in at first. After serving a customer, she saw him from the corner of her eye. She walks over to him from behind the counter with her great big smile. She welcomed him to Pop's Place and asked how she could assist him when she realized who he was. Harriet was glad to announce that Eric was the mall Santa and how they needed some holiday cheer in the place because of the mood that was there. Eric cut her off in the middle of her sentence. He let Harriet know with an attitude she would not get any holiday cheer from him. He asked if he could get a drink without the sweet sugar and spice personality or would that be a problem for her. Surprised by the slight disrespect and tone, she raised her left eyebrow and asked what he was drinking. Eric asked for a tall glass of rum and cola but held the rum, a twist of lemon, and a cocktail umbrella to keep it dry. This was Eric's way of making the mood light. He knew this lady did not deserve that and even more, not his personality. Well, it worked. Thank the Lord.

Harriet joked that he had a soul in him, and it was not as crushed as she thought. Eric apologized and let her know he was having a terrible day. Eric knew who Harriet was but still asked her what her name was. He knew more about Harriet when she was a child, but as she got older, he did not get to interact with her as much. Harriet Renfro, she told him, and she was the owner of Pop's Place. Eric, recalling a memory, asked her if she still collected race cars and how she never, ever asked for dolls for Christmas. She told him she did still collect and went into detail about a Classic 1977 Stingray she got one year. Then she wondered how he knew this and asked Eric. He looked down at the soda she put down on the counter in front of him. He avoided eye contact and told her from her father. Eric let her know he was sorry to hear of his passing, and her dad was a good man. With a smile, Harriet thanked him for his kind words and told him not to be sad. Her father left her with the tavern and a load of great memories of Christmas. She told Eric a story of how one year her father forgot to make Christmas cookies. With the biggest smile and some giggles that he instead made some grilled hot dogs and left those instead for Santa with mustard, relish, and ketchup, Eric interrupted her in midsentence by saying they had no onions on them.

Harriet laughed and agreed with him about the no onions. She asked did her father tell him this story before. Eric with a slight smile told her yes, and he was an "onion on a hot dog kind" of guy. Harriet had to go to serve another customer. As she left, she told Eric to hold on to that holly jolly smile, showing on his still-red cheeks. Eric, feeling better, thought to himself how Harriet was a good kid, but then again, she always was. This all happened before Tina and I arrived at Pop's. We were two stores away from loading the last few gifts to take over to the church for wrapping and distribution at the service later in the mall. That is where Billie met us to help. I told the ladies we had one more stop before we headed back to the church. We had to get the toys wrapped and ready for the service later. I joked we could not leave Santa short on gifts.

Tina laughed and added we had to help get his sleigh down the hill. We thought it was funny, but Billie stood there, puzzled. She had to say something because she did not get this. Tina thought she was drunk and asked what was wrong with her besides the obvious.

Billie explained, "Supporting Santa Claus and toys is what's wrong. Knowing this season has nothing to do with any of that."

Tina did not think Billie was serious and was ready to ignore her and told me I should do the same. After she saw Billie's face, she realized she was serious. Billie went back to her sharp wit and to get back at Tina, told her she was as serious as that ugly hat she had on her head. Billie then turned to me and asked why we are doing this, knowing people will not look at God but a man—a man. It is something I have thought about for years.

I told her I saw her point, then I added to the conversation by asking what the deal was.

I told them how each year I prayed on Christmas that people would see God and not the holiday extras. And each year, things seem to get worse—the shopping, the people and the prices. I did not understand how or why people let him take a back seat to the toy man. But then one day, in prayer as I prepared for Bible study, God spoke to my heart about this situation. I had Billie's attention, but Tina was still in a joking mood. She then asked me what happened and did the cactus on my desk catch fire and speak to me. Billie scolded Tina and told her to be serious for once in her life and told me to go on with my story. It surprised me because she wanted to hear what I had to say.

I began by saying, "He told me to look beyond the things and stuff, but look at the reasons for everything. Jesus was the gift that keeps on giving. God's gift of his son was a sacrifice on his behalf. With this gift, we were to duplicate it and carry it on in our everyday lives, and Jesus was the perfect example, showing love to those who are in need, giving of yourself and not looking for a thing in return, always honoring your parents and elders and being a father to the fatherless and a friend to the friendless, also having hope for the hopeless, praying for one another, and getting his Word across with the message of love. That is what we support, Billie. We do this to help those in need this time of year, and by doing this, it shows all the things we are to do like Him. So yes, we give them gifts, but it's not just that or the food, toys, and entertainment. We show them Jesus and the gift of His love, and Santa, a man doing God's will."

I know Tina got it because she was clapping and praising God. But Billie looked more like a child that got scolded. I asked her what was wrong, and I saw a tear roll down her cheek but then this gigantic smile. She told me she never thought of it that way, and for the first time, she understood. Billie then asked me what else we should do. I told her we needed to pray and be honest with the Lord when we do. Billie took it a step further and asked what we pray and how do I pray as the pastor.

"Hmmm," I told her, "Usually, I pray on Christmas and that the Lord will see me through. I pray for his wisdom and to show me what to do and that as I walk my daily path, he leads me and advises me. And I pray for a constant hedge of protection over family, friends, and congregation."

Billie took a moment to absorb the words I spoke. Then said she understood, but she would have to follow up when she came to service tonight. Tina and I were both surprised but thanking God! We gave Billie a group hug and prayed with her. I never expected this, especially with her, but with God, all things are possible. This was the seed; my prayer is that Billie gives herself to Jesus 100 percent. But as the old hymn says, "One day at a time, sweet Jesus." I asked the ladies to take the gifts to the church so they could start wrapping them and I would stop at Pop's to grab the last few toys and meet them in twenty minutes. They said their goodbyes and took the van of gifts down the road as I made my way over to the tavern.

Chapter 10

Fire on Ice

I hope that I did not put you to sleep so far, but this is the part when the day got interesting and very much out of the ordinary. I walked into Pop's, and you could tell it was not the same place. The mood was gloomy, not the right setting for Pop's and on the holiday too— no way! There was one glimmer of hope shining through the fog, and that was Harriet, who waved to me as I came in the door. I tried to lighten the mood by yelling at her to get me a gin and tonic. I love to shake up people, the gasps, and murmurs that the pastor asked for an alcoholic drink. Harriet laughed and called me a silly man. She reminded me and the others I am not a drinker and the gifts I came to collect were over in the corner. I apologized to the folks because I should sustain from appearances by even making them think I drink. But with this sad group, I had to shake them up, and that was too good to pass up. The people still groaned and some laughed as I walked toward the box where the toys were. But as I walked, I noticed Eric sitting over at the counter. I thought it was rare to see him there at the counter, let alone at all on Christmas Eve; it was his busiest day of the year. I walked over to him and told Harriet that there was a face I did not expect to see here, then I asked, "Santa…is that you?" But Eric turned away from where I was.

I joked for him not to have that much to drink, reminding him he had to drive his sleigh to the mall tonight. As I reached to put my hand on his shoulder, Eric ducked under it to avoid contact, noticeable to everyone sitting at the counter. Something was wrong here, and I let it go. In my mind, I wanted to know what his issue was; this was not the time or the place. I reminded everyone about service at the mall tonight. I hoped to see them all there, but not any responses from the group. Then from the end of the counter, David, the businessman, asked me what time service was. He then said he could not be with his family this Christmas, but he would not be without God either. I felt my spirits pick up a bit as I told him service was at eight o'clock. I also wanted to see what I could do to help, to regard the situation with his family. The only cure he knew was to fly him to his loved ones tonight somehow. I told him we could not do that, but we are all family in Christ so come worship with his brothers and sisters.

Harriet assured David and me she would make sure he got to service tonight. You can always count on Harriet coming through in helping people, just like her dad! Did I say how much I missed Harry? I told them how great it would be to have them there as I picked up the bag of toys and headed to the door. I leaned on Eric's shoulder as I passed by, saying that Santa would hand out gifts and it would be fun, still in a way trying to get his attention, and I got it all right!

In a stern, almost-growl, Eric questioned, "Will it really be fun, Pastor? *Really*!" David, who was sitting at the other end of the counter, came to my defense. He told Eric that all I said was it would be fun and what his issue was. Eric then snapped at David, asking him, "Fun, yeah, but for whom, you jerk?"

The next thing I knew, Harriet and I were getting between these enormous men arguing. David suggested that Eric had too much liquid cheer for the night talking to him that way. Eric came back at that remark by letting him know he had a whole glass of cola soda pop and to take his keys. I tried to get Eric's attention by asking him could I talk to him. I moved him back to his seat, but in the back of my mind, I was thinking, *Someone call 911*. I, again, said to Eric, "Can I talk to you? Can I tell you something?"

Eric raised out of the seat and told me something. He called me by my first name Reggie, not Pastor Reggie or even pastor. *Trouble coming*, I thought.

He told me how tired of this season he was and all that goes with it. "People don't care. So why in the world should I? So in conclusion, find yourself another Santa because I am not coming tonight or any other night. Christmas is canceled, and *I quit!*"

Eric slammed his glass on the counter and walked out the door into the frosty early evening air. Everyone stood there in shock—no one more than me. I also felt like the people who were there were looking at me as "What did you do?" It was like I got him upset and made him quit. Lord, forgive me, but that angered me beyond belief! Here was this man in my face, scolding me as if I was an opponent in the ring. I thought to myself, this was no wrestling show promo, and I was not some pushover, fall guy. I dropped the toys right on the floor to follow him out the door. Before I chased him up the hill, I had to make a phone call. I called Eric's wife, Selina. She could make some sense out of whatever was going on, but even if she did not, she needed to know of this odd behavior. When she answered and we talked, I could tell her spirit was not right. She seemed as confused as I was and had no explanation for the behavior. Selina also told me she's upset about what transpired at the house when he left, also being reminded about their son Chris. I told her he was on his way up to Amour Flats, which is a small woodsy area overlooking the mall, and I went after him to talk. I told her everything would be okay, to pray first, and to meet me there in fifteen minutes.

She told me later that after she got off the phone, she immediately went to her knees in the kitchen and prayed. "O Heavenly Father, I am thankful for all you have done for us, but I need you now more than ever. Eric needs you now more than ever. He has grown so tired and bitter toward this season and has forgotten the joy and meaning. He needs to know you still love him and have not forgotten him or his purpose here. I don't care about gifts, the business, or even the mall. I want the loving, joyful man of God you gave me. Help us both to get back and carry on your joy and peace. Please?"

After her prayer, Selina grabbed her keys and coat off their hooks and headed out the back door to the car. I told her to meet me in fifteen minutes, but I knew it would not take her that long, so I hurried to catch Eric. As I recalled the events of the night and with the extra information from Selina, I was trying to put the puzzle together. How Eric could have changed so, but I realized for a pot to boil over, it had to be stewing for a while. By the time I caught up to him, I was upset. I did not know if it was because my friend was having troubling thoughts or because he did not talk to me about it—from the way he treated me in the tavern to how he has me running up this hill! I don't like running or hills or running up hills! I finally saw Eric, and he was sitting on a rock near a tree that gave the best view of the mall and the town. I called his name, and he did not answer or even move, which did not help with my attitude. At that point, I must have been crazy or thought I was a two-hundred-and-fifty-pound wrestler. I grabbed Eric by the arm and pulled him up off that rock. I spun him around, and we looked at each other, evil eye to evil eye. This was the making of a great wrestling pay-per-view.

"Angry man!" That was what I called him. "What is going on with you?" I asked if he was ready to face me now or run away again. Eric talked back to me, asking what did I want, did I want to take a hack at him? Now I was bugging out and ready to go into a collar and elbow tie-up as they do at the beginning of a matchup.

I told him, "Yeah. I want a piece of you, Jack. What is all this? Your attitude stinks. I would say you have a huge chip on your shoulder, but it is more like a redwood tree, and nobody knows why. Not even your wife, who you left as you stormed out of the house this afternoon. And yeah, I know about it." I brought my tone down. I told him she was worried sick, and I know he felt it. I was still angry. "And yeah, I want a piece of you," I told him again. "Who are you, man?"

Chapter 11

The Great Reveal

Eric took two deep breaths, like a Brahma bull ready to charge. He looked down on me as if he would break me into fifty pieces and scatter them in the woods. Did I say I should have called 911? Anyway, instead, Eric turned to face the sky, "I am fed up with who I am… pulled like taffy. Everything is gimme this and gimme that, do this or do that. Taking everything I got, and for what…holiday cheer? Blessings? No, for their own selfish reasons."

I then had to ask Eric what he was talking about. Even better yet, who was he talking about? I reached up to put my hand on his shoulder and prayed because I could see and feel my friend was getting very bitter. I began by asking my Heavenly Father to help my brother in this time of need. Eric turned around to face me and interrupted the prayer.

"Him too, everybody and *him too*!" Eric was very direct at this point. There was no compromising with him, but I knew this was not him, so I asked what was going on here. Eric became very calm and remorseful and told me how he felt forgotten, and even he seemed to forget what the holiday was all about. I was sad to hear what he was saying. I wanted him to get it out. I let him know I was listening. We had all the time in the world for him to explain. It was he and I. Eric opened up.

"What is this holiday about, this time of year, no one seems to know anymore. The focus is on what you get for what you gave, how much for what price, who you can step on or over to get what you want. The thing is, there is no difference from the rest of the year.

Yes, I should be happy. My delivery service picks up 100 percent. But when you deliver to the people now, you don't even want to give them their package. You know, I wish my son would go into the business. It would give me some relief, but don't tell Selina I said this. But he *is* better off where he is…*happy*! I realize that, but the old man still wished he did. But I don't want him to have to deal with these people. So where is God in this, Reggie? Why does he allow this, or did he forget me?"

I felt his pain, his questions, and his heart, everything… Here was this hulk of a man baring his soul and asking for answers. At that point, I teared up, and in my head, as we stood there, I told the Lord I could not do this and asked how I could help him. And quicker than it had time to resonate in my head, I heard Jesus speak to me: Matthew 21:22, "And all things whatsoever ye will ask in prayer believing, ye will receive."

"So what do you believe, Pastor? And pass it to your brother."

I cried more, but now for joy. He gave me what I asked for the both of us.

"*No*…no, Eric. He has not forgotten you now, especially because he uses you. By your actions and not words, you live Christ. People are deceived, but it is up to us. You…me, and other believers to let people hear and see God in us. But for you…let me refresh your memory of what this holiday is about. Eric, the one gift, God's gift already given that stands the test of time, is Jesus. There is nothing better, and no way can we out give that. His sacrifice for our sins is beyond measure. God sent his only Son to die so we may live. That is what this is all about. So when you give, it is out of love for others, to meet needs, to show how much you care…to show just who and what God is…through us. That is why you do what you do…not because of what the season is but *who* is the reason for the season."

Eric, then crying himself, picked me up and gave me a giant bear hug. I could feel my ribs touching my spine. Okay, and yes, I am exaggerating, but it was a tight grip. He apologized for being an idiot and got on himself about forgetting what was important. Eric wanted to go back to Pop's to apologize to the guy he was ready to punch out. I thought that was a good idea, but then we both heard a voice coming from the trees behind us. Unnoticed by us was the fact that Harriet and David had followed us up to the flat. David had the same apologetic thought in mind himself and wanted to fix it. Then everyone got a good laugh as David told Eric it was a good thing that he did not hit him. He was a heavy bleeder. David also explained he understood Eric. How he was so wrapped up in missing his family, he did not thank God for even having a job to provide for his family at Christmas. Harriet then let them know that God forgives us, and so should we forgive each other.

Eric and David then shook hands and apologized to each other. Now that's what I needed to see. Then from the corner of my eye, I saw Selina, who also heard the conversation we had. I looked at my watch and made an excuse about how late it was. We all had to be at the mall within the hour for service, but before Eric left, he had to make amends with one more person. I directed him over to the other side of the flat where now Selina was standing.

"See you at service, Santa," and I walked toward David and Harriet who also then made excuses. Harriet remembering she had to lock up for the night. David went with her to make sure she was safe while closing. Eric walked over to his wife and hugged her, apologizing for his attitude.

Selina quieted her husband and spoke, full of love and understanding, "I heard the complete thing. I did not know what was going on in your head. You men always keep things to yourselves and let them build until you explode. We could have discussed this. God created me to be a helpmate for you. You could have let me know you did not recall what the holiday was about anymore. I would not have judged you but reaffirm what you already knew…just forgot."

Eric then let her know that was it. It upset him he forgot about God's gift of Jesus and what He stood for, what He came for. He, for a moment, questioned if Mary herself even knew what she was about to do in that manger. They stood on there for a moment, staring at the now-crisp black and blue starry sky. They again hugged each other. A big sloppy kiss is what I expected before they made their way down the hill toward Pop's. Eric called the warehouse on his way down. He told them to prepare for the night and have someone meet them in the parking lot. He had to run an errand before he went to the mall.

As they were walking into the lot, they saw Harriet and David headed for her car. Harriet noticed them as well and excused herself to ask if they were going to service tonight. Eric answered her with a big smile and a resounding *yes*! He asked David if he needed a ride tonight. David thanked him but advised that Harriet would take him to service tonight. Eric looked at Selina, and they both laughed, which puzzled Harriet.

"Oh? Do you think Harriet's little yellow bug will get you home to Sarah, Davey, and Rhonda?"

David took a step back, asking Eric what he said. He never met this man before tonight, let alone told him about his family. Before he could get another word or thought, out two of Eric's delivery trucks pulled up to them in the lot. Then three little men jump down from the cab of the trucks. The one driver tells Eric, "We brought everything as he said." Another handed Selina a box. He tells her that the route changes he requested are now in the mapping system. Now I was not there. But Harriet says that the back door of the first truck opens. Out of the truck come eight reindeer, and the driver puts them in a two-line order, four on one side then four on the other. The other truck opens, and out rolls this huge sleigh, red-trimmed in gold with a green garland. As Selina dressed Eric in his famous red suit, he told both her and Harriet, that he had to make a stop at the mall for service and the kids. Afterwards, he could drop David at home between his trips to China and Alaska. Amazed, Harriet and David could not believe their eyes. Mentally, they turned into their five-year-old selves. Harriet, though, with a bit of disbelief, asked if he was Santa, the real Santa. All Eric did was touch her on her nose and gave her a hohoho. She realized now how he knew about her car collecting, her dad, and the no onions hot dog and told her he was an onion kind of guy. David, now realizing that he was Santa as well, had more to digest because he was going home to be with his family. David gave Eric the hug of a lifetime, thanking him for the greatest gift ever. Eric took no credit and told him to think of it as an answered prayer. God answers prayer.

"Now lets go to service," Eric said, "but remember."

Harriet chimed in "I know, don't tell anyone your secret. Then Eric told her "Yes, but tell everyone about Jesus."

He then reached in his pocket and pulled out a package and gave it to Harriet and told her Merry Christmas. When Harriet and David got into her car, she opened the package—to find a picture in a compact frame from 1979. It was of her and her dad, Harry, with the car she was missing from her collection that year.

Chapter 12

Reflecting during the AM

Well, it was two o'clock in the morning now on Christmas day, and I found myself still up. I sat here in my kitchen, thinking of the events of the night and how unexpected they were. The first thought is when I locked the front door of the mall after everything was over. I had a conversation with my Heavenly Father. "Well, this has been quite a day. Jesus, you sure had a birthday bash of the ages in this town. For the first time, the church did not have to buy anything for our service or celebration. People came through and gave so much. We had gifts and food to spare. Even after donating to the senior center, the children's hospital, veterans' center, and homeless shelter. But twelve people dedicated their lives to you today. Hallelujah, Father! You were here today, tonight, walking among us, fellowshipping, and the worship service was off the hook. Wow! I know I am not making any sense, Lord. To be in your presence and see your wonders is overwhelming, even for a seasoned follower like me. I must admit, it worried me earlier today. Things were falling apart for tonight. As far as attendance, gifts, food…Eric. I did not know what to do. But in Psalms 55:22, your word says, 'Cast your cares on the Lord and He will sustain you. He will never let the righteous be forsaken.' And look at you keeping your word, but, Father, I am confused. Eric is Santa Claus? Eric, Santa…Santa, Eric? I don't get it!"

Then I heard, in a booming sound, a voice that called my name, "Reggie!"

I dropped to my knees in reverence and asked Jesus was it Him. Was he finally going to talk to me? Then I heard, "Turn around, Pastor!"

As I slowly turned—wait, it was not God—it was Eric, a.k.a. Santa, standing behind me. He helped me up. I guess I looked as if I would pass out. He came back to talk to me, and this is what he said, "I know this was a surprise to you. Heck, sometimes I struggle to believe who I am and what I do is only a carbon copy of God the Father. He gave the ultimate gift of his Son for us. The gifts I give only stand as a reminder of how great a gift God gave and the joy you should have received it. There was joy, peace, salvation, and love beneath that Christmas star. And I go out to remind people of that each year. So it is not me they see each time. It is the Christ in me, and remember this, my friend. If he could use Noah who was a drunkard, Abraham who was too old, Isaac a daydreamer, Jacob the liar, Moses stuttering, Gideon who was afraid, and Lazarus the dead man…why not Santa Claus? So the question you should ask the people is, who do their beliefs belong to?"

"Amen, my brother, *amen*" was all I could say at that point.

He was so right and blessed me in the process. He even gave me a ride and flew me home. Crazy, right? The second blessing being is what happened toward the end of the night at the party. I still don't understand, but I am not complaining. One thing my mother always said, "Always be on your best behavior. You never know who is watching." And I found out how true she was. So what am I referring to? Well, the party ended, and we were all cleaning up the area in the mall we were in. Santa and Mrs. Claus—well, Eric and Selina— were still greeting and thanking the guests for coming.

Tina and her cousins were wrapping up the leftover food to send to the shelter. Billie, after helping the musicians break down their equipment, went over to help Harriet break down the boxes from the coats we gave away. Billie even blessed us with a miniconcert. A night of miracles! Anyway, let me stay on track. I was using the dumpster cart to pick up the last of the boxes and trash. I went over to where Harriet and Billie were to get the boxes. No big deal, right? I guess I was standing there for a minute because Billie came over and asked me if I was here to pick up boxes or eye strain. She also said for me to ask the girl out, referring to Harriet. I ignored her and grabbed the boxes. Harriet was very gracious, thanking me for my help, but me again, not realizing this time, just stared. Billie then tells me the cart is full, and I should empty it. I guess in a way she was helping me, but as I left, she was making a kissy-face motion out of Harriet's eyesight to taunt me. As I walked past the boxes to the dumpster, I wondered if I was too awkward and what Billie was saying to Harriet.

When I came back in, I walked over to where the stage was and had a seat. From where I was, I could see Billie was talking to Tina and her cousins, and Harriet was with Selina. Again, I must have been staring at Harriet for a moment because I did not feel Eric tap me on my shoulder. He asked to have a seat and then asked what I thought. I said everything was awesome and how much God blessed us. He agreed with me and said he always does. Then he asked me why I didn't go talk to her. I asked him who he was referring to, then he dropped Harriet's name. I told him, "No, sir," but then he came back with the question of why I should not. I gave him the only excuses I could think of about being friends and how I was her pastor. How would that look?

Eric said, "Well, like a man who found his rib."

Confused, I asked, "His rib? What?"

But he was referring to Adam and Eve, the creation of a helpmate. Eric then broke it down for me in a way I never thought or never noticed before—how I needed someone to look out for me, to love and pray, to help me with a ministry. Then he talked about his wife, Selina, and how God made her for him and how they both knew that. He told me not to dwell on a past relationship, it was not my fault, and it was settled.

"But you know in your heart, Harriet is God's choice for you. Without asking, she is always there for you, always helping when she can while still running her own business. Best of all, she has a personal relationship with the Heavenly Father. Come on, Reggie! If you stare any harder, you could go blind."

He was right, and I had to agree. Even if—and that's a big *if*—I was thinking about it, I did not know what she would say or even what to say to her. Eric saw my doubt and asked questions like, "What was her favorite food?"

"It's pepperoni pizza with cauliflower crust."

"Then what was her favorite ice cream?"

So I answered, "The mint chocolate chip."

"What did she wear last Sunday?"

"It was a blue dress with a black belt and high heels. She was wearing pearls too."

At that point, Eric told me to stop. He wanted to know if I was serious. He didn't even remember what Selina wore last Sunday. I realized he knew I had it bad for Harriet. So did I. Eric then got up and went to pick up his Santa sack and came back to his seat. I thought it was empty; it looked empty, but he pulled out one wrapped package. I asked if it was for me as he handed it to me. He told me no and to look at the tag. The tag reads,

To Harriet,

Merry Christmas.

From Reggie

The tag matched the red wrapping paper and green bow and ribbon. I told him I did not remember buying this gift, forgetting who I was talking to, still all hard to believe. He told me to stop talking, pay close attention, and listen. Eric told me about the gift he was giving to me. He and Selina invited Harriet over for Christmas dinner, you know, once he got back from his run. He said to offer Harriet a ride when I come over myself. So I questioned him about me coming to dinner because this was the first I heard this. Again, he told me to stop talking and to offer to bring her to our house and give her that gift. Can I do that?

I then agreed because I actually could do that, so he asked, "Why are you still sitting here then?"

I got up and thanked Santa and made my way over to Harriet. As I walked, I could see Selina leaving Harriet by herself. As she walked past me, Selina looked at the gift in my hand and gave me a wink as she went over to her husband.

When she made it to Eric, she asked, "Did you think it would work?"

Eric said yes. In his mind, he was hoping it would.

So when I got to Harriet, it was like she was waiting for me, or I was hoping she was. I told her I wanted to thank her for all her help with tonight's events and putting things together. She was very gracious, letting me know she loved helping me and the church. There were some awkward pauses and slight glances and smiles. I looked over to see Eric and Selina looking at us. Eric gave a nod as they turned and walked out the side door.

I told her the Kerfees invited me to dinner, and they invited her. I then threw caution to the wind and asked since we were both going if she would mind if I offered to bring her. Harriet looked at me and questioned as if she did not hear my request to pick her up but then smiled and said yes. We set the time for two o'clock and said our goodbyes for the night. I turned when I remembered the gift I had in my hand. I asked her if she would not mind, but I got her a little something for Christmas and gave the gift to her. I told her I hoped she would like it, and she said I was sweet for the gesture. She read the tag and tore open the red paper, eager to see what it was. Before she even finished opening it, she stopped. Harriet stared at the gift and cried. I still could not see what it was, but it could not be good. Now I was feeling bad. I apologized to her and offered to return it. Instead, Harriet grabs me around my neck, plants a kiss on the cheek, and thanks me five times in a row. If you are confused now, you know what I was feeling. She then stepped back and took off the rest of the paper. I finally got to see what it was. The gift was a wrestling action figure, mint in a box. A rare, hard-to-find Deacon of Danger figure—her father. If I was not there, I would not believe it myself, but it happened. God is awesome! It was now three fifty-five, and I now have a very blessed and busy day ahead. It would be hard to get to sleep, but I must try. Lord, I ask you to forgive me.

You know what is best for me better than I do. All you ask is to trust, obey, and listen. When I did not focus, things seemed to be falling on me, on everybody. It was the faith of a few you instructed that kept hope alive. You used that beautiful vessel, Harriet, to help see you and your plan. I ask you Lord, to help me honor you today as I try not to make a fool of myself around her. Thank you, Father, and good night... Amen!

In Memoriam

Dr. Marcel Lynette Johnson
Bishop Melvin L. Rodgers DD, PhD